THIS BOOK BELONGS TO:

....

For Lenka.
E. L.

Copyright © Tiny Owl Publishing 2021
Text © Elizabeth Laird 2021
Illustration © Toby Newsome 2021

First published in the UK and US in 2021 by Tiny Owl Publishing, London. With special thanks to Knights Of Publishers for their support.

For teacher resources and more information, visit
www.tinyowl.co.uk

#GloriasPorridge

A catalogue record for this book is available from the British Library.
A CIP record for this book is available from the Library of Congress.

UK ISBN 978-1-910328-68-2
US ISBN 978-1-910328-72-9

Printed in China

GLORIA'S PORRIDGE

ELIZABETH LAIRD
TOBY NEWSOME

TINY OWL

Gloria was making porridge.

Her cat was watching her.

"I like porridge," he said,
winding his tail round Gloria's legs.

"Well, I'm sorry, Cat, but you can't have any," said Gloria. "I'm hungry and I'm going to eat it all myself."

The porridge took a long time to cook.
"It's too sticky," said Gloria.
"It needs more water."

She picked up her bucket and ran down
to the stream to get some water.

The cat crept up to
the porridge pot.

"It looks very good," he thought.
"I'll just lick a bit off the spoon."

The porridge tasted so delicious that he ate some more, and then a bit more, and a bit more after that, until all the porridge was gone.

Soon, Gloria came back from the stream
with her bucket of water.

"Oh! What's this?" she cried.
"My porridge pot is empty!"

The cat was washing the porridge off his whiskers.

"You see, it was like this, Gloria,"
he began to explain.

But Gloria wouldn't
listen. She frowned
and shook her
spoon at him.

The cat was scared of Gloria's spoon. He ran out of the house with a loud meow, and jumped on to the back of the donkey, who was having a nap underneath the tree.

"MEOW!"

"HEE HAW! OH AAH! YOU'RE TICKLING ME!" laughed the donkey,

and he began to frisk about all over the place,
shaking the tree till the leaves all rustled.

Up in the tree, the bees in the beehive were busy making honey.

"Why is everything shaking?" they hummed.

"Buzz! Hmmm!" they buzzed.

They flew down out of the tree and zoomed about in a panic.

The hen was laying out her corn on a mat to dry.

"SQUAWK, SQUAWK! CLUCK, CLUCK!" she cackled.
"Here come the bees! What if they sting me?"

She flapped her wings in fright, scattering her corn everywhere.

"OH, WHAT A FUSS!
OH, WHAT A BOTHER!"

Gloria was shouting, and the cat was meowing, and the donkey was braying, and the bees were buzzing, and the hen was clucking.

The fox was passing by.
"What's going on here?" she asked.

Everyone stopped and
looked at each other.

"The bees frightened me and made me
flap my wings," said the hen.

"And my corn flew about all over the place,
and now I've got to pick it all up again."

"We didn't mean to scare the hen," said the bees.
"But the tree started shaking so we flew out
of our beehive."

"I shook the tree," said the donkey.
"The cat tickled me and made me laugh
and jump about."

"I was running away from Gloria," said the cat. "I was scared because she was shaking her spoon at me."

"Yes, because you ate up all my porridge," said Gloria."

"But I'd been chasing mice for you," said the cat, "so I was hungry too."

"Never mind all that,"
said the fox.

"What are you going
to do now?"

Everyone looked
at each other.

"I'll go back to picking up my corn," said the hen.

"And we've got our honey to look after," said the bees.

"I need another nap," said the donkey.

"I'll say sorry to Gloria," said Cat, "because I ate up all the porridge."

"And I'll say sorry too," said Gloria, "because I was too greedy to give any to my cat."

So off went the hen,

and the bees,

and the donkey,

and Gloria, who
made another
pot of porridge.

When it was cooked, she gave some to the cat, who wasn't *quite* full, and after they'd eaten it all up they sat down under the tree for a rest.

And the cat climbed up on to Gloria's
knee, and she stroked and stroked him.
And everyone fell fast asleep.

But the fox just smiled her clever
smile, and went on her way.

ELiZABETH LAiRD

Elizabeth Laird is a multi-award winning author of many successful picture books and young fiction. Her travels across the world have influenced her style of writing and choice of topics. She is well-known for tackling a wide range of global issues through her work. During the 1990s Elizabeth collected folk stories from traditional storytellers in Ethiopia and the British Council produced them in a series of readers for Ethiopian schools. *Gloria's Porridge* is a retelling of one of those folk stories.

elizabethlaird.co.uk

TOBY NEWSOME

Toby Newsome was born in Cape Town, South Africa in 1975. He studied Graphic Design and started a career as a freelance illustrator and book jacket designer. Now he mainly works on editorial and children's book illustration. He plays the guitar - mostly finger-style folk music and lives in a very beautiful city, surrounded by the sea and a mountain. Toby loves hiking and feels lucky that he can walk to the forest from his home. Toby's illustration style is colourful, graphic, and whimsical. He loves pattern so that often features in his work. The South African inspired illustrations for *Gloria's Porridge* translate this story into a pan-African fusion.

tobynewsome.com